BOOK 5

JAN AND THE SECRET CAVE

THE ITURIA CHRONICLES

J.B. MOONSTAR

BOOK 5

JAN AND THE SECRET CAVE

THE ITURIA CHRONICLES

J.B. MOONSTAR

DEDICATION

This book is dedicated to the Audubon Society,
as well as the many other researchers and scientists, in appreciation for their continuing efforts
in researching and protecting the wonderful birds
that inhabit this Earth, including their efforts to
save the few remaining Chinese Crested Terns, the
"birds of legend." Thank you!

Dear Reader,

One of Ituria's main goals is to rescue endangered animals, saving them from death at the hands of man. In my continuing chronicles of the interactions between Ituria's realm and the human world, I will relate the story of a young girl and her courage to protect those who need her help, even if the likelihood of success seems impossible.

On Earth, Chinese Crested Terns are extremely endangered and at one point had been declared extinct. Discovering an expedition is studying a group of these terns, Jan joins them with her father to help him with his research and see if she can do anything to protect them. While at the nesting site on the cliffs, she finds a small silk bag in a cave that starts an adventure with many unexpected surprises.

When she learns poachers have stolen many tern eggs, she is determined to rescue them, and with a little help, to transport them, along with their parents, to Ituria's Island where they will remain safe. But what chance does a young girl have against a band of poachers?

Sincerely,

Knocker,
First Guard to Ituria

Table of Contents

Chapter One

LOST IS FOUND

Tiptoeing carefully around the cluster of nests atop the cliff, Jan followed a narrow path so she wouldn't disturb the birds sitting on their eggs. Ahead of her, she could see the cave entrance she found yesterday; the small silk bag she'd discovered there was calling her back! What else could she learn about the small carved figure she found inside?

Taking the figure of out of its bag, it was only about three inches tall. A man, his left hand pointed down to the left, while his right arm was bent at the elbow, clutched fist resting on his chest. His frozen gaze followed his pointed fingers.

"What are you doing here… and where did you get that?!" came an urgent whisper behind her.

Jan jumped, almost dropping the little figure. Turning around, she noticed Knocker just a few feet away, nimbly jumping over one of the egg-filled nests to reach her. The terns didn't seem to mind him; perhaps they were used to his presence. Knocker was tall and lean, over a foot taller than Jan, although not much older. She figured he was about 14 or 15. When he finally reached her, he grabbed her by the shoulders. She looked up at his face, his bright green eyes were wide with surprise as he repeated, "What are you doing here?"

"Do you know what this is?" Jan asked, holding the figure up. "I found it yesterday in the cave, and I wanted to see…"

"Look," Knocker interrupted. "You can't be here now." Even though he was whispering, his voice was tense. Taking the statue from her hand, he quickly put it back in the bag and looked around, making sure no one was watching. "It's too late to return to camp now. They're almost here. You must hide in the cave and not come out—no matter what!"

"What's going on? Why do I…" Jan started.

"No time to explain—they will see you, now *run!*" Knocker quickly put the bag in her hand and turned her toward the cave. "Go!" he commanded. "I'll keep them distracted so you can reach the cave!"

Knocker turned and immediately headed in the direction he had come. Jan could hear shouting, but she didn't understand what they were saying. She also heard growling. One of the people Knocker was yelling at must have a large dog. Knocker had never seemed so stressed before, so she heeded his warnings.

She ran quickly inside the cave and hid behind the rocks at the cave entrance.

Sitting in a dark corner and hidden from the outside world, she held the bag tight, feeling the little stone man inside. *What could this be about, and why is Knocker up here?* He was usually out with the other researchers on the lower cliffs, documenting the tern nests and identifying which were Chinese Crested. There were only a few dozen of the Chinese

Crested Terns nesting among thousands of the Greater Crested Terns, and she was just learning to tell them apart.

Shouting from outside grew louder, and Jan pressed further back into the cave, hiding as best she could. The dog's growling grew louder too. *It must be an extremely large dog.* Angry threats were exchanged; Jan didn't need to speak their language to understand the tone and message. She would stay hidden until Knocker told her she could leave the cave.

What is going on? Why is Knocker here now, and who is he yelling at? Jan thought back over the past few days. She came with her dad to research the Chinese Crested Terns, known as the "bird of legend" since they had returned from near extinction. Knocker was there when she and her dad arrived a few days ago, and he was helping with recording their numbers. He tirelessly worked from sunrise to sunset, keeping up with the thousands of birds seeking nesting spots on the cliff.

Of course, his real name wasn't Knocker. That was his nickname; his real name was Marcus. When he was younger, he would knock into things. So when people started to call him Knocker, the name just stuck. He liked the name; he said it fit him. *But what is he doing now? Why is he outside yelling—and at who? And what does this little stone figure have to do with any of it?*

Jan's wandering thoughts were cut short—hearing footsteps running toward the cave. She crouched lower against the cave wall. *I hope it's Knocker!*

Chapter Two

A Mystery Unfolds

A few moments later, Knocker appeared at the entrance. "Jan," he called quietly into the cave. "It's okay to come out now."

Jan jumped up from the cave floor and ran out. *It is dark in there!* "What's going on?" she asked, still worried about the yelling she heard just a few minutes ago.

Rather than explain, Knocker turned and strode down the path. Looking over his shoulder, he called back to her. "We can talk as we return to camp."

Running to keep up, Jan was still waiting for an explanation.

"Listen, you must be careful," Knocker turned his head so she could hear, "and never come out alone on these cliffs. The people I was talking to were poachers. They are here to steal the tern eggs. I managed to chase them off for now, but they will be back. Egg stealing is an easy way to make money." As the path grew a little wider, where they could walk side by side, Knocker asked, "Where did you find that little statue?"

"I found it in that cave," Jan explained. "I was up there with my dad yesterday, counting the terns when I wandered into the cave and peeked inside." Removing the bag from her pocket, she continued, "It was sitting beside some rocks. I briefly saw a shimmering light when the sunlight reflected off the silk bag; that's what caught my eye."

"Do you mind if I look at it again?" Knocker asked as he slowed down, just a little, giving Jan enough time to remove the figure from the silk bag.

Opening the small bag, she reached in and brought out the tiny figure. She looked at it again, turning it over in her hand. "Look!" she exclaimed. "There's something on the bottom! I didn't see that before." Then, she put it in Knocker's outstretched hand.

"So it does, and you found it in that cave?"

Knocker stopped walking to look at the bottom. The drawing was a crescent moon and what looked like an apple. "Can I see the bag, too?"

"Sure," Jan said as she handed over the small silk bag, sparkling as the threads caught the sunlight. "What do you think it is?"

Knocker examined the bag, inside and out, and his fingers felt the smoothness of the pure silk material.

"Well," Knocker replied, suddenly serious, "this looks to be between three and four hundred years old. The drawing of the moon and apple remind me of a story I've heard numerous times."

"Really! What is it?" Jan wanted to hear more, to learn the story behind it.

They were only a few minutes from camp; however, Knocker stopped walking and sat on a large flat rock along the path. He motioned Jan to sit beside him. "Let me tell you what I've heard." Knocker's voice contained a hint of excitement. "I thought it was just a fireside story, but maybe there is more to it."

Jan looked at him and waited for him to continue.

"Many years ago," Knocker started, "some say hundreds of years, maybe thousands, there were stories of a Nymph named Lilya who was appointed by the Goddess Hesperides to tend to one of the golden apple trees in her garden. When she thought no one was looking, Lilya stole one of the apples and ran away. Knowing that Hesperides would be looking for her in Europe, Lilya hid in the East Asian islands. It is rumored she hid the apple or its seeds in one of the many island caves, leaving clues so she could return to find it once the Goddess grew tired of searching for her."

Jan waited for more. *What did the statue have to do with anything?*

As he continued, Knocker held up the figure. "Look at the bottom of the figure, the sign of the moon and an apple. Do you think it could lead us to the golden apple?"

"How can we tell?" Jan asked, hoping there was a way to follow the clues.

"Well, we can go back after lunch while the others are gone for supplies," Knocker replied, his voice revealing he was truly intrigued by Jan's find. "Can you show me exactly where this was in the cave?"

"Of course!" Jan replied excitedly.

Knocker's voice grew serious again as he looked at the small figure. "However, first you must promise not to tell anyone about this, not even your father, until after we check it out, okay? We don't want treasure seekers flocking to the island while we are researching the terns." Then, looking directly at Jan, Knocker asked, "Can you do that?"

"Yes, I promise. Not until after we check for more clues!" Jan said, nodding.

"Okay, then," Knocker said as he stood. He handed her the stone figure and turned toward camp, "Here you go. Keep it safe. Let's return to camp and check in, then we can head back after lunch."

Jan carefully placed the figure back into its bag, then safely tucked it into her pocket. *I can't wait for the adventure to come!*

Chapter Three

READY TO EXPLORE

Arriving back at camp, Knocker and Jan were met by Jan's father.

"Jan!" he called out in a worried voice. "Where have you been? I've been looking for you. You shouldn't be out there alone."

"I wasn't alone," she replied quickly, glancing at Knocker as she added, "I was with Knocker."

"She's safe, George," Knocker added. "I was with her atop the cliff. I agree… she shouldn't be out there alone. You and Russell must know I saw three people who looked like egg poachers on site earlier today. I chased them off, but we need to be extra vigilant. The poachers will grow more daring since they now know there are eggs for the taking."

"Agreed. We are going out for more supplies now, Knocker," George responded. "I know this is your last day with the group, but do you think you can stay tonight until we get back? I don't want to leave Jan alone on the island while we are gone."

"Yes, I'll be glad to," Knocker replied. "We'll change the pick-up time for a few hours later, so I should be here until this evening."

"Thank you, Knocker." George reached out and shook Knocker's hand, grateful that he had agreed to stay. "I will feel much better knowing you are here this afternoon."

"Don't worry, George," Knocker replied. "I'll make sure she is safe."

Turning to Jan, George continued, "Bye, Jan dear, we're off now and will be back as soon as we can. I'll bring you some fresh bread if we can find any at the local market." He gave his daughter a hug and a quick kiss on her forehead, then turned and climbed aboard the small boat they used to travel back and forth to the mainland.

"Bye, Dad. Please be careful!" Jan called out, waving to him.

He waved back. "Will do! You be careful too and stay with Knocker while I'm gone, okay?"

"I will, for sure!" she called back with a smile, anticipating the adventure ahead.

As the research team leader—Russell—was about to join George on the boat, Knocker called out to him, "Russell, while you are in town, can you please contact my ride and tell them we need to change the pick-up time for later tonight. Maybe around nine? I must stay here for a few more hours."

Russell looked at Knocker for a second, thinking to himself, then nodded and replied, "I will contact them as soon as we reach the mainland. You must leave by nine o'clock. Remember … you have other duties at another site starting tomorrow, so it can't be later than nine!"

"I remember," Knocker responded, nodding. "I'll make sure to return to camp before sunset, so I can wrap up my research notes and arrive at the pick-up site on time! Thanks, Russ, I appreciate it!"

Once the boat was on their way, Jan turned back to Knocker. "What now?"

"Let's have a quick lunch, then we can grab a few flashlights," he replied, heading toward the food tent. "That way, we can go back and see where this little guy was pointing."

Jan and Knocker entered the food tent and made a quick lunch of cheese and fruit, each lost in their own thoughts on what secrets awaited them once they returned to the cave.

"That was delicious!" said Jan as she stood, eager to head out. "We will need energy for exploring the cave this afternoon. Thanks for helping me try to solve this mystery!"

"I'm glad to help, and I'm very curious as to what we will find," Knocker replied. "Hopefully, we won't see any more poachers! Wait one minute while I grab my bag," Knocker called as he turned toward his tent to grab his duffle bag. "You never know when you will need to carry something!"

Jan nodded, remembering that Knocker usually worked in the field with his duffle bag, and it always had what she needed—paper, pens, nets—whatever the situation called for. *Good idea to bring it along!*

"I'll grab my backpack also. Between the two of us, we should have everything we need!"

Jan ran to her tent and grabbed her backpack, meeting Knocker at the edge of the camp, ready to head back to the cliff at site three, eager to solve the mystery of what else might be hidden in the cave!

Chapter Four

THE
SEARCH FOR CLUES

❧

Eager to return to the cave, both Knocker and Jan walked quickly, heading toward the cliff where the figure was found. To get there, they would have to walk past the area where the poachers were last seen by Knocker.

As they walked past, Knocker said, "We must be careful, okay?" His voice was hushed and serious, his eyes moving quickly as he searched the surrounding area for any remaining poachers on the island. Also, he looked out over the inlet, seeing if any boats were heading toward them.

"Once we reach the cave," he continued, "don't wander far. We must stay close together since we don't know what is hidden there. I need you to show me exactly where you found the bag and how it was positioned. It seems the figure was pointing to something in the cave."

"Right, that's what I was thinking, too," Jan replied. "But what could it be?"

"That's what we need to discover!" Knocker answered as they took their first steps into the cave.

The cave itself had a small entrance, forcing Knocker to lower his head as he entered. The noon sun was bright, providing some light into the cave for about five feet or so. Anything beyond the reach of the sunlight was dark and unknown.

Jan walked over to the left wall, which was three feet inside from the cave entrance. Then, she took out silk bag and looked at it, remembering the first time she saw it. The material was a light blue flower on a black background woven brocade; it measured about three inches wide and six inches long with a silver binding and tassel. A small dark-red bead was sewn in to hold the tassel in place. The sunlight caught the light blue coloring, and the silver binding and tassel glimmered like a little sparkler in the darkness.

Glancing quickly back to the cave entrance to get her position, then looking over to the left wall and floor, Jan carefully positioned the bag on the floor, tassel side up, making a right angle to the wall. Several small stones blocked it from view if someone had tried to glance into the cave from outside.

Yesterday, she had stepped into the cave entrance, and the sunlight caught the silk material and silver binding, just like it was doing now. Was it just by chance that it hadn't been found for hundreds of years?

"Okay," Jan said as she pointed to the bag. "That is what I saw yesterday. See how the sunlight catches the blue and silver?"

"Yes, I do," answered Knocker, nodding. "I have been to this cliff several times, but never saw the bag. I can see now that you must be positioned exactly just inside the cave entrance to find it. Do you remember how the figure was arranged in the bag when you found it?"

"Yes, I think so." Jenna went over and picked up the bag again. "When I opened it, I removed the little figure and it was pointing this way." As she spoke, she opened the bag and pulled the statue out; the hand was pointing into the cave toward the darkness. Setting it into a standing position atop the bag on the ground, it pointed to another rock a little further back, just barely visible in the darkness.

Jan and Knocker moved quickly toward the other rock. Knocker clicked his flashlight on so they could both see what might be waiting for them on the other side.

Once behind the rock, they saw a small clay vase with a stopper in the top. It was covered with a thick layer of dirt, almost blending in with the dark coloring of the rock it rested against.

Knocker picked up the vase and walked into the sunlight at the cave entrance. "What do you think is in here?" he asked as he brushed the dirt off.

"I don't know," Jan replied. "We'll need to clean it up so we don't break it when we open it or whatever may be inside."

Jan reached inside her backpack and took out a bottle of water. She slowly poured small amounts water in one area, wiping it with her hand, then carefully removing one layer of dirt at a time. After a few minutes of cleaning, the outside of the vase was visible.

"Amazing!" Jan exclaimed. "Look at the drawings on this vase. It looks like a painting!"

"Yes, but a painting of what?" Knocker asked, slowly turning the vase in his hands. It was about fifteen inches tall and eight inches wide, each side having a different painting on it, four in all. The paint was old and faded, but the shapes of the paintings remained, a dark rust color against the tan color of the vase.

"The first could almost be an apple tree. See the trunk and branches and the little fruit circles?" Jan asked. "The second looks like an outstretched hand saying, stop or wait." Jan turned the vase to the third and fourth drawings. "This looks like a dragon breathing fire!" she exclaimed, pointing to the third drawing. "Do you think this is a warning to keep people from entering the cave?"

"I'm not sure," Knocker replied as he continued to examine the vase.

"What do you think the fourth drawing is?" she asked. "I can't make it out."

"It's possibly a map of the cave, or perhaps it is saying the map is located inside?" he replied.

"The only way to find out is to open it," Jan added. "How can we can do that without breaking it? It looks tightly sealed."

"We may have to break the seal, but first … let's make a sketch of the paintings, in case we need them later." Knocker took out a small notepad and pencil, then drew the four figures. "I'm not positive we have accurately identified the figures, but this should help later on."

The fifth drawing atop the stopper gave Jan a shudder. It was a large X on what looked like a fallen man covered in flames. *What could this mean? What danger were they getting themselves into?*

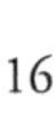

Chapter Five

FINDING THE MAP

Removing a pocketknife from his bag, Knocker worked on the stopper, trying to loosen the years of dried clay used to seal it closed. Although it took several minutes, he was successful in chipping out the stopper seal. "Are you ready?" he asked Jan, looking at her, his hands ready to open the vase.

"Well, I am getting a little worried," she replied softly with slight hesitation. "What if there is danger in the cave, and by opening this … we are summoning all the bad things painted on here: a fire-breathing dragon or a man being burned? Should we be doing this?"

"I'm not worried about a dragon," Knocker said. "However, I am worried about the fire part. It's in two of the paintings. It's possible this cave used to be part of an active volcano, so when the drawings were made, there may have been a hot lava flow below. However," he continued, "if we want to solve the mystery of your little figure, we must enter the cave. If the map is in here, it will help us navigate the cave."

"Okay," Jan agreed, still uncertain if they should ignore the vase's warnings. "I'm sure glad you're here with me. It's better not to explore dark caves by yourself." She took a deep breath and smiled at Knocker as she said, "Let's do it!"

"Okay, here it goes!" Knocker replied.

Tapping the stopper around the outside, Knocker separated it from the vase.

A strong, musty smell rose from the vase opening, and Jan could believe it was indeed several hundred years old. Knocker tipped the vase on its side and turned it toward the light, peering in to see what it might contain. Gently, he removed a small scroll. The material was very delicate; just touching it caused several tiny pieces to flake off.

"Hold on a minute!" Jan called out quickly. "I've got an idea!" She removed a large zip bag from her backpack and laid it on a flat part of a nearby rock.

"Now, carefully unroll the scroll and slide it in here. Then, we can zip the bag flat and smooth out the air, so that we don't lose any more pieces."

Knocker did as instructed, slowly unrolling the scroll until it was mostly flat. Jan held the bag open, and Knocker gently slid it into place. While it laid on the rock, Jan carefully flattened it and pushed out the air, then zipped the bag closed, forming a perfect, air-tight seal. "Now if we can keep it from breaking apart in the bag, we'll be good!"

"Let me draw what we can see now," Knocker added. "So if it does fall apart, we will still have the contents of the scroll. It looks to be drawings also, but it does looks like a map."

Knocker studied the map as he drew the markings on another sheet of paper.

"Look!" he said with excitement, pointing to the various drawings on the map. "Here is the cave entrance, and the rock where we found the vase. I wonder where it leads?" Knocker said, as he gazed into the darkness at the back of the cave.

After another few minutes of drawing, he pointed to several parts of the map and added, "This shows we need to take a sharp left turn, go down another twelve to fifteen stairs and cross a room, then turn a sharp right into another stairway. I hope the stairs are still there and in good shape!"

"What is that?" Jan asked, pointing to a section of the map beyond the stairs. "It's the warning hand and the big 'X' on a fire. Is it a warning to stay away? And here," she continued pointing to another section, "this looks like the dragon drawing again."

"But look here," Knocker replied, pointing to the bottom of the map. "It's the tree drawing again with an apple on it." Finishing his drawing of the map, Knocker continued, "Let's take this one step at a time and evaluate each section as we get to it. If it looks too dangerous, we can turn around. We can't let our curiosity put us into danger. Okay?"

"Sounds like a plan!" Jan agreed. While she felt a little scared, she really wanted to find out the secret of the figure in the bag.

Knocker looked toward the back of the cave again, seeing total darkness. Taking a quick glance at his watch, he turned to Jan and said, "Okay, it's 12:15 p.m. now. We must get moving if we plan to return before sundown tonight."

Carefully rolling up the map, now sealed in plastic, Knocker put it back into the vase. He then put the vase in his bag to keep it from breaking. They could use his drawings for their map and pull out the original if there were any questions.

"Okay, let's go!" Knocker called to Jan, "and remember to stay close!"

Turning his flashlight on and pointing toward the back of the cave, they headed in, using their flashlights to search for the first sharp turn left, marking the beginning of their descent.

Chapter Six

DOWN THE LEFT STAIRS

Leading the way, Knocker shined his flashlight into the darkness, trying to find the staircase going left. The light hit what looked like a small hole in the ground, and closer inspection showed it was a small, very tightly wound staircase carved into the rock.

"Let me go first," Knocker said. "Then stay right behind me. I will use my flashlight to show the steps, and you use your flashlight to show the walls. This is a very narrow space, and I don't want to hit my head!"

"Sounds good!" Jan agreed. Taking out and turning on her flashlight, Jan stepped closer and put her hand on Knocker's back. She would be watching the walls and wanted to make sure they were moving at the same pace.

Every few steps, Knocker would stop and take a deep breath. After the third time, she asked, "Are you okay?"

"Oh, I'm fine," he responded. "When I am in a dark place, I use my sense of smell to help me prepare for whatever we may find. Currently, there are numerous smells, but they are mostly mushrooms and an underwater stream. We're good for now!"

Jan took a deep breath. She only smelled humid, stale air filled with the dust they were stirring up as they went down the stairway. Knocker must have been trained to separate all the different scents he identified.

After shuffling fifteen stairs and ducking several times to keep from hitting their head on the staircase, they reached the bottom. Knocker took a small step into the room and shined the flashlight around the area, trying to figure out what was next.

"The floor here feels solid," he said. "But the map had some funny markings to follow. Here, look at this."

Jan stood beside him as he shined his flashlight on his drawings. It showed two different types of tiles, one with human-shaped feet and the other with animal-shaped feet. The tile with the animal-shaped feet had a big X through the middle.

"This must mean we can only step on the human feet tiles," Jan determined. "What do you think?"

"That sounds right, but look at the tiles now," said Knocker as he shined the light on several of them. "How will we tell which is which?"

Looking at the tiles as Knocker lit them up, Jan could see that the cave floor was indeed covered in tiles from wall to wall. However, there was a thick layer of dirt over them; you could just see the small indent in the dirt separating the tiles. They would need to clean each one to make a path; this was going to take a while.

Jan looked back at the drawings on Knocker's map. "We don't have to clean the whole tile," she said. "Look." She pointed to the drawings. "If we clean off the top, then we can tell if the footprint has the toes of the human footprint or has claws like the animal footprint."

"Good call!" Knocker said. "And the path is kind of marked here on the map. It looks like two blocks on right diagonal, then turn left into some sort of zig-zag."

"Let's clean based on this map. We only have to clean the toe part so we can see if they have toes or claws. That should save a lot of time!" Jan cleaned the first tile per the map.

"This looks like a human foot," Jan noted to Knocker. "Now, should I go left or right, up or sideways?"

Knocker took a quick glance at his drawing and said, "Go on the diagonal, right, then up. Make sure you stay on the human foot tiles, though. I don't know what will happen if you put any pressure on the animal footprints. I suspect it probably isn't good."

Since each tile was about twelve inches wide, Jan was able to stay on one tile while cleaning part of the next one. Knocker was standing behind her, shining a light down on the floor so she could see the tile she was cleaning.

Slowly working their way across the tiles, Jan started scrubbing on a tile that at first glance appeared to be a human footprint but wasn't. After the first scrub on the tile, it broke apart and fell into a pit beneath—there was no cave floor under the animal tiles! Several seconds later, the sound of tiles breaking on rocks echoed, telling them it was a long fall if you went through the animal claw tiles. *We must be careful!*

Making sure not to put any pressure on the animal claw tiles while cleaning the human foot tiles, it took about half an hour to get across the room. Once across, Jan noted, "Well, at least it should be easier to leave, since we've already cleaned the path!"

"I hope you're right!" Knocker replied, looking at his map. "The map doesn't show anything about taking a different path out. And look over to the right." He shined his flashlight to the right of the cave. "It looks like the second staircase."

Chapter Seven

Down The Right Stairs

As they approached the next stairwell, Jan's flashlight shone on the wall beside it, revealing a large painting of a fire breathing dragon and a hand signaling them to *stop!*

"Do you think there is a dragon hiding down here?" Jan asked, not quite sure what to believe at this point.

"Don't worry, Jan, I've got that covered," Knocker replied with a slight smile on his face. "To be safe, once we go around the first turn and make six steps, let's turn off our flashlights. If there is anyone down here, they won't be able to see us, okay? I'll tell you when."

"Do what?" Jan asked with great alarm at the suggestion. "Turn off our flashlights? But we won't be able to see either! How will we get down the stairs? What if there is someone down here? How would we know?"

"Use your ears and nose, your sense of touch. Let your other senses guide you. But please maintain your hold on my back so we don't get separated, okay?" Knocker then took a deep breath, in and out, remaining silent as he evaluated the new scents.

"I smell something here that isn't a mushroom," Knocker whispered. "We must be on our guard now. Don't talk or make any sounds. I don't want any surprises."

Nodding her head, Jan took up her place behind Knocker and put her hand on his back. Her flashlight lit up the walls so they wouldn't hit their heads; his flashlight lit up the stairs so they wouldn't make a misstep and fall.

After three steps down, Knocker paused and took another large breath.

Another three steps, another large breath. Taking a second deep breath, Knocker turned off his flashlight. Reaching back, he tapped Jan's flashlight, signaling her to turn hers off also. They would go in total darkness.

Jan was really worried now. "Are you sure?" she whispered. "How will we see what could be down here?"

Knocker whispered back, "We don't need to see. I can smell what is down here."

Slowly descending a few more steps, Knocker called out in a loud voice, "Greetings Dragon, I am Knocker, First Guard to Ituria. We have come in peace! We will not harm you. May we enter your lair?"

Jan thought Knocker was pulling a trick on her, calling out to a dragon. He said before he wasn't worried about there being dragons here, so he must be joking. She waited for him to turn the flashlight back on and laugh. That thought quickly vanished when growling and a roar came from the room beyond the staircase. Now she was scared. *There really is a dragon down here!*

"I have come to return the apple tree to its owner and free you from your oath!" Knocker responded to the growling.

Knocker slowly took another step down. At this point, Jan was in panic mode and put both hands on Knocker's back. She didn't want to lose him in the dark. *What is happening? Who is he talking to? What is growling back?*

Remembering from earlier today, the growling she heard now sounded like the large dog she had heard when Knocker was chasing off the poachers. *Perhaps the poachers are down here with their dog?* That was the only thing she could figure out.

Another step down, one more step toward the growling.

"We have come to rescue you. May we enter?" Knocker called out again.

Tapping her foot on the floor before her, Jan confirmed there were no more steps down. The floor was now level. At least they didn't have to worry about falling down a staircase in the dark.

As their eyes adjusted to the darkness of the bottom room, Jan saw a faint golden glow coming from the other side. It was in the shape of a small tree. *There is a magic tree down here!*

However, between Knocker and the magic tree was a large dark object blocking their way. She couldn't see what it was, but it was alive and moved as it growled at them in response to Knocker's attempts to talk with it.

Knocker took another step toward the dark object, a large shadow against the tree's faint light. Jan continued holding onto his back. Suddenly, the growling turned into a voice, a female voice. "I smell a human. Prepare to fight!"

Jan gasped and turned to run away. Knocker quickly reached back and grabbed her arm, whispering, "Jan, stay. I will protect you."

"What's happening?" Jan whispered in panic. "Who are you talking to?"

"Please stay for just a few more minutes," he whispered back. "You are safe with me."

"Megan," Knocker called to the dark shadow. "If I return the tree, then you are no longer bound to kill all humans. You will be free!"

"I am bound to defend this tree against all humans, and you have brought a human with you!" Megan yelled back at Knocker.

"I am here to free you from your oath. If I take the tree, then it wasn't taken by a human. You can leave, your oath satisfied."

The shadow moved toward the tree, almost blocking its golden glow from view. "Knocker, First Guard to Ituria, I can never leave," the voice said quietly, sadness filling her words. "If you take the tree, my only light in this cave, I will be in total darkness."

Chapter Eight

MEGAN'S STORY

"**M**egan," Knocker answered. "I don't understand. Why can't you leave? If the tree is gone, you are not under oath to protect it."

"When I was brought here, I was a small dragon, captured by Lilya. She chained me to the wall. I have been here for so many years, I don't know how long anymore." Megan was despondent. "Even if you can break the chains and free me from my oath, I am too large now to escape."

Jan wasn't sure what was down here, but whatever it was, it needed their help. Still holding on to Knocker's back, Jan whispered, "Knocker, can we help her? Is there any way to get her out?"

"Let's see what we are up against," Knocker responded. "Megan, is it okay if we turn our lights on in here so we can figure out how to break you free?"

"Whatever you wish. I have not moved more than a few feet since I was put here."

"What do you eat?" Jan called out into the darkness, wondering how this creature could have survived here for so long.

"Lilya, being a tree nymph, planted some magic mushrooms that provide me with full nutrition, and there is a small stream running nearby that provides water to us both—me and…*her tree*." Megan's last words showed her total resentment toward the tree. "If not for that tree, I would not be here. Yet, it gives me the only light I have in this dark cave, so I cannot destroy it."

Megan voice was breaking as she revealed her tragic story. "She promised to only be gone for a few days; she promised to return … but that was so long ago. She left me here … forgot about me." Her voice trailed off into silence.

As Knocker clicked on his flashlight, Jan's eyes were briefly blinded as they adjusted to the light again. Then she saw Megan.

She could hardly believe the sight before her. A large slender dragon appeared in the circle of the flashlight as Knocker moved it first to Megan's face, then to her body. She was 18 to 20 feet long, ruby-colored scales sparkling in the light, and with large, dark grey wings folded against her back. Her forelegs were crossed in front of her, and her left back leg was chained to the wall. Her head was resting on the ground in front of her forelegs, and tears were flowing from her eyes.

"Why would she just leave me here? Why?" Megan asked sadly, knowing neither Knocker nor Jan would be able to answer.

Knocker shined the flashlight on her back leg, trying to trace the chain. The chain was embedded into the skin on her leg, since she was now much larger than when she was left here.

"Megan!" Jan stammered. "You really are a dragon!"

Megan lifted her head and snorted a little at Jan, not happy to see the human girl. As she regained her composure, she turned to look at Knocker.

"Knocker," Megan said. "Why did you bring a human down here?"

"Megan, let me introduce you to Jan," Knocker said as he pointed to Jan. "She is the reason I was able to find you. She found the clues, leading us to the map, and then finally … to you."

Megan looked at Jan again, apprehension filling her voice. "I'm not sure if I owe you a debt of gratitude or should curse you for stealing my only light. Only time will tell how I will remember you."

So many things were swirling around in Jan's head. Megan was a real dragon, and she was talking to her. *Wait, how can I…* "How can I understand you now?" Jan asked. "I only heard growling before. Knocker, you heard the growling too, right?"

"You haven't told her, have you?" Megan said as she turned to Knocker.

"No, but she will learn soon enough. I will have to explain all to rescue you from this cave." Turning to Jan, Knocker said, "Jan, it may make more sense if I tell you while relating the part of the story Megan doesn't know."

Turning back to Megan, Knocker continued, "I know half of your story, Lilya's half. And you may not even know that part of it as I doubt she would have told you."

Knocker walked over until he stood between Megan and Jan.

"Many years ago, Nymph Lilya was requested to care for a magic apple tree whose fruit greatly prolongs life. The tree was given to Ituria from the Goddess Hesperides; a gift of encouragement when she learned of Ituria's plans to rescue animals and transport them to the moon."

"On the moon?" Jan asked with disbelief. *This is getting crazier by the minute.*

Knocker looked at Jan. "Yes, Ituria and I live on the moon, technically in the caverns under the moon's surface. We travel to the earth to rescue animals that need our help, such as the Chinese Crested Terns. That is what I am doing in this research group."

"So … you travel back and forth to the moon, carrying animals?" Jan asked in disbelief. "So how do you get to the moon?"

"I will explain later," Knocker said, then turning back to Megan. "Now back to Lilya's story."

"Lilya was requested by the Goddess to stay with the tree to keep it healthy. After about 1,000 years, Lilya missed being on Earth, so she stole one of the apples for its seeds and left the moon. Once she left the moon, they never heard from her again. No one knows what happened to her. Legend says she told someone she had left a map to find the apple seeds, and the only way to find her prize was to find the little figure and follow the clues."

Looking back at Jan, Knocker noted, "That was why I was so interested in the little figure you found. It could have been the clue Lilya left behind."

"Megan, does this fill in any of the gaps in your story?" Knocker asked.

Megan nodded. "Yes, your story explains a lot. Lilya had a small tree she planted here in the cave, granting it eternal life, and allowing it to generate its own light, so all it needed was water from the stream."

"But why did she have to leave you here, Megan?" Jan asked, trying to follow the story line.

"She caught me as a small dragon and made me swear to protect her tree from all humans. She said she would only be gone a few days, promising to return and stay with me down here … but … she never came back." Megan's voice cracked, and she dropped her head. "Why did she leave me here?"

"Has anyone ever been down here?" Knocker asked.

"Only an occasional fish in the stream, which I would talk to and play with," Megan replied dejectedly. "While I may live for thousands of years, fish have very short lifespans, and I have grown accustomed to living alone, as there was never any alternative."

"Knocker," Jan asked again. "Can we help her? Can we set her free?"

"I see two major problems we need to overcome, and to do so, I need two things," he said. "One, Megan I will need your complete trust." Turning to Jan, he continued, "Jan, I will need your oath that you will not reveal anything you may see here to any human ever, not even your father."

"What do you mean, 'not to any human,' what about you?" Jan exclaimed. "Can I talk about it with you?"

"Well, yes, you can," Knocker replied. "You can talk to me about it whenever you want, because I am not a human."

Chapter Nine

FREEDOM FOR MEGAN

"Okay," Jan said. "Now I know you are fooling with me, right?"

Knocker looked at Jan, thinking of how best to explain the current situation. "First things first, Jan, and then I will explain." Knocker then said to Megan, "Megan, my solemn dragon oath to you, I will free you from these chains and allow you to reach the surface, setting you free from this cave. You may live on Ituria's Island should you desire, without fear of human intervention. In exchange, I request to return the tree to its rightful owner, Ituria."

"Knocker," Megan said. "My solemn dragon oath to you, you may take this tree to its rightful owner, and I will not harm your human. You have my trust, though I do not see how you can free me from this cave."

"Jan," Knocker said, "this will answer your question also as I explain to Megan my plans to free her. Please shine both flashlights on the chains on Megan's leg so I can focus on them."

Jan did as requested and aimed each flashlight at Megan's back leg, including the chain attached to the wall. "Are you saying you're not human? That makes no sense! If you are not human, then what are you?"

Knocker walked over to the chains and lifted several links off the ground with his hand. "As Megan can tell, I am a dragon in human form. I have the scent of a dragon. That's how Megan knew I was not a human. Even in human form, I have the strength of a dragon and can break these chains. Megan, please stay still, and I will try to do it with as little discomfort to your leg as possible."

Holding the chains slightly off the ground, Knocker, lifted his right foot and slammed it onto the chain. The links bent, and after a few hard stomps, the chain broke. Megan's leg was no longer attached to the wall. Free, but still too large to climb the small staircases.

"So, you are a dragon, just like Megan?" Jan asked in disbelief, still trying to figure this one out.

"Yes, that is correct. And now, for the second part," Knocker said. "This may take a little explaining. I have a magic potion that allows me to transform at will into a human. It lasts for seven Earth days at a time and will wear off at 9 p.m. tonight. That is why Russell and I were discussing that. I must leave camp by 9 p.m. or risk the others learning my secret."

"What?" Jan said, astonished. "Is Mr. Russell a dragon too?"

"No, no, no. Russell is human," Knocker answered. "He is part of Ituria's Alliance here on Earth. Last week, he told me the terns would be laying eggs this week. In the past years, many of the freshly laid eggs were usually stolen by poachers before they had time to hatch. I am here to prevent that from happening. When I saw you on the cliff today, I had to change my plans and scared them away. However, they will be back. They are probably back on the island above us already, after watching your dad and Russell leave for supplies."

"Megan," Knocker said, turning to her. "You have given me your trust, and I will not break it. I have a spare potion in my bag I can give you. Since I know you have been here for about 350 years, you will take a human form about my size, maybe a little smaller. Big enough so you can climb the stairs to the surface. I am 465 years old, so this is the size I am when I turn into a human."

Jan stared at Knocker in disbelief. *He is 465 years old? He is a dragon? What else will I learn about him?*

"But I was told to kill all humans. I can't become one!" Megan cried out. "How can you bear to be human? All they do is kill dragons! Even I know that!"

"Megan," Knocker said softly, pausing for a moment before continuing in a solemn voice. "I understand your fear completely since humans killed my mother." Knocker briefly closed his eyes as he remembered that painful day.

Jan's mouth opened, but no words formed to express her shock at Knocker's revelation. *His own mother was killed by humans!*

"Yet," Knocker said as he continued his story, "Ituria rescued me and took me to his Island, where I have lived for over 400 years. During this time, I have learned there are good humans too, not just murderers. Jan is a good human. She is trying to save the terns who nest on this island."

"Who does she need to save them from?" Megan asked. "What are poachers?"

"Well, as I said," answered Knocker, "Jan is a good human. She respects all life." He paused, shaking his head. "But there are those who have no respect for animals and will kill them for profit. They do not care what damage they cause to animals or their families. The poachers I refer to steal eggs from the nests and sell them in local markets."

"If you take my potion, we can leave this cave," Knocker continued. "We could use your help to rescue any eggs that may have been stolen, then transport them, along with their parents, to the moon. It will take our combined effort to retrieve the eggs and get the parents together before it gets dark."

Looking at his watch, Knocker noted, "It is now 1:30 p.m. It will take at least forty-five minutes after you transform to leave this cave, and we need to return to camp before 7:30 p.m. when the researchers return from their supply run."

Reaching into his bag, Knocker produced a small, glass vial shaped like dragon tooth. Carefully removing the stopper, he held it out to Megan. "This will transform you and allow you to leave this cave."

Megan reached out and accepted the vial; it looked tiny in her giant front claw. She held it gently so as to not crush it and looked back at Knocker. She did not drink it yet, still a little uncertain to Knocker's plans.

Knocker continued, "Once we reach the opening, we will most likely run into the poachers again. I know this is asking a lot of you since we have just met, but you should know … I will keep my oath to free you whether you say yes or no. It is your decision to make, whether to help us or not. However, I need to know your decision now, so I can plan our actions once we reach the cave entrance. Will you help us?"

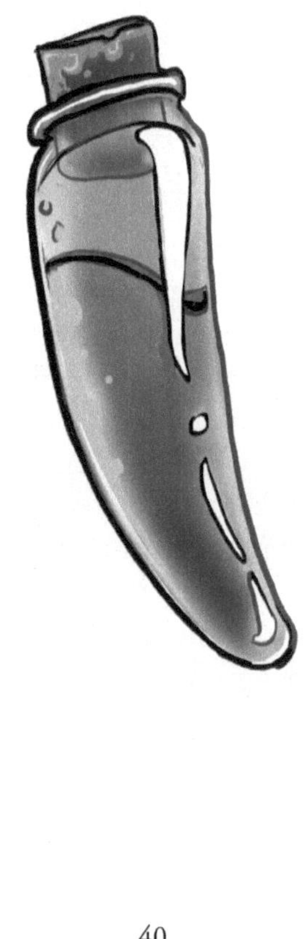

Chapter Ten

LEAVING THE CAVE

Megan briefly looked at Knocker, then at Jan, then back at Knocker. Nodding her head, she quietly answered, "If you free me and let me live on the moon away from humans, I will do everything in my power to help you rescue the terns and succeed in your mission."

"Thank you, Megan." Knocker bowed to her. "I appreciate your help and will ensure you are transported to the moon with the terns and their eggs." He pointed at the small vial in Megan's claw. "This is what I take, so you can trust that it won't harm you. I give you my word. You must allow the transformation though, so you must accept that you will be a human, at least for a little while. You must remain calm until you get out of the cave, as if you transform back into a dragon before then, you may be hurt by the small stairways. Do you understand?"

"I will do my best," Megan replied. "But I do not know what will happen when I turn into a human. How do you deal with being so small?"

"You will get used to it," Knocker said. "It will only be for a little while until we get you out of here."

"Okay," Megan said. "I will do my best to stay calm, at least until I can see daylight again. Whatever happens, I want to thank you both for your efforts to rescue me. Without you, there is no telling how much longer I may have been down here. Thank you." Megan bowed her head to both Jan and Knocker, then drank the potion. Her eyes looked worried as she handed the empty vial back to Knocker.

"So… what happens now?" she asked, still doubting the potion's ability to work.

"Megan, just remain calm, and let the transformation take place," Knocker encouraged. "It won't take long once you let it happen. Focus on good things, like leaving this cave and returning to the sun once again. In the meantime, I will go pack up the tree for its return to Ituria."

"I will focus on being in the sun once again, to feel its warmth on my skin," Megan responded calmly and closed her eyes.

"Jan," Knocker called to her. "Your role in this mission is just as important. You asked how you can now understand Megan. Well, it is because I have this stone." He took a stone from his pocket and handed it to her.

Jan looked at the stone, a small stone about the size of a half-dollar coin. "What do you mean? What is this?"

"This is a rare translation stone that belongs to Ituria. It allows humans to understand non-humans. You must be within about ten feet of the non-human. If they are farther away, you will only hear their natural talk, like you heard Megan's growling from earlier." Knocker started walking away from Jan. "This will make sense when I get more than ten feet…" he said. Then all Jan could hear were growls, like the large dog she thought she had heard before lunch—*it had really been Knocker!*

Knocker leaned over and picked up the small tree, making sure a clump of dirt remained to contain its roots, then placed it into the vase they had found earlier. He was careful to fit the roots inside the rolled map, so they both fit perfectly together, neither one damaging the other. He started growling to Jan again as he headed back.

As he got within ten feet, his growling turned to words. "…here, Jan, you will need to hold this tree. When we reach the surface, I will need my bag to store the eggs we rescue from the poachers. If it will fit into your backpack without damaging the tree, that will work."

"So, you were the growling I heard earlier. That was you yelling at the poachers! Now I understand!" Jan briefly took out the stone and looked at it, then carefully placed it back, so she wouldn't lose it in the cave.

"Yes," Knocker said. "That is correct. Since I was more than ten feet from you, the translation stone didn't work. You heard my natural voice; the poachers heard a human voice." Looking at the vase with the tree in it, he continued, "Do you think this will fit in your backpack?"

Jan took off her backpack and carefully put the vase and tree inside. If she didn't zip the top, it fit well, only a few branches sticking out the top. "This works," she said as she put the backpack on her back.

"Ah, Megan!" Knocker reacted as he saw her in the glow of his flashlight. "You have been successful! Good job! As I said, transformation is all in your mind—a calm mind controls the body."

Knocker walked over to the now human Megan, extending his hand to her as she sat on the ground. "Let me help you up. It will take a few minutes to get used to walking on two legs, so please hold onto my hand or Jan's as we go up the stairs."

Megan reached up and took his hand, using it to steady her as she stood. "I feel so small right now." Her human form, revealed in the flashlight, was of a tall, slender girl around twelve or thirteen years old with long, dark grey hair, wearing a ruby red dress.

"Megan," Jan said. "You look just as beautiful in your human form as you do in your dragon form. I'm so glad we were able to find and rescue you. At some point, I hope you will understand that I really do want to help."

"Jan, I do understand," Megan replied, "and I am grateful that you and Knocker have extended me your kind assistance. I will be eternally thankful to you both."

"Jan, you have the tree and translation stone," Knocker noted, "and once we reach the surface, you will have an important task to perform. You will need the translation stone, so please put it in a safe place for now, so we don't lose it climbing the stairs."

Jan checked her pocket and confirmed that the stone was safe. "I've got it," she said. "Now let's get out of here! Knocker, you take the lead by using your flashlight to light the stairs. Megan, you can go between Knocker and me. Place your hand on his back. I will remain behind you to steady you as you climb the stairs. I will shine my flashlight straight ahead so we can see where the ceiling rocks are."

The trio headed to the first stairs with Megan balancing herself between the two, still learning how to walk on two feet. "I'm sure I'll get this walking on two legs down soon, but for now, thanks for keeping me steady!" Megan seemed happier already, allowing the prospect of leaving this cave to finally sink in.

POACHERS RETURN

Crossing the tiles and up toward the second set of stairs, Megan started walking with more confidence. She was able to balance on two legs while she walked, even climbing the stairs.

Upon exiting the second set of stairs, Knocker turned back and put his finger to his mouth, signaling Megan and Jan to be silent. Taking several deep breaths, he whispered, "Jan, the poachers are outside the cave now. This is the plan. Megan and I will scare them away and follow them to rescue any eggs they may have already been taken. Your job is to go to where the nests are and talk to the birds."

"How am I going to talk to the birds?" Jan asked, not sure how she could do so.

"Remember the translation stone? As you get within ten feet of the birds, you need to call out to them, and they will understand you. This is what you will need to say, over and over, as you slowly walk down toward the rock we stopped at before lunch today. When you reach them, call out and say 'If your eggs are gone, follow me. Knocker, First Guard to Ituria, is rescuing your eggs from the poachers and will take you and your eggs to safety. Please, if your eggs are missing, follow me!'"

"Are you sure this will work, that they will understand me?" Jan repeated.

"Jan, if you can understand me now, then when you are within ten feet of the birds, they will understand you," Knocker explained. "You must repeat this message as you head toward the rock. Wait until the poachers are gone, then start. You must use all the words, including that you are working with me—Knocker, First Guard to Ituria, so they can identify who you are."

"So that's why the terns were never afraid of you!" said Jan, finally realizing why the terns always stayed in their nests whenever he approached them. The terns always scattered whenever she or any other member of the team tried to get close to the nesting grounds. He was able to talk to them and explain why he was there! *It was finally making sense.*

Pointing to Megan, Knocker continued, "Megan and I will leave first and meet you at the rock after we secure the eggs and put them in this bag. Any questions?"

"No, I don't think so," Jan replied. "I sure hope this stone works!"

"Megan," said Knocker. "I would prefer to stay in this form when we confront the poachers. It will cause less of an issue. However, if needed, please be ready to transform back into a dragon and defend yourself. It will be easier than transforming into a human. Just focus on being a dragon—that's all it takes! I have learned the humans outside will have no problems trying to kill us if it means successfully stealing these eggs. Just follow my lead, okay?"

Megan nodded. "Knocker, you have earned my complete trust, so whatever you think is best, that is what I will do."

"And, Jan," Knocker said, "remember … once we are separated, you will not understand what we are saying. We will depend on you to bring the birds to the rock. It's almost 2:30 p.m. now, so we are running out of time."

The three reached the cave entrance. "The moon will be bright tonight, which is a good thing," Knocker said as he looked at no one in particular.

What does he mean by that? Jan wondered.

"Okay, Knocker, First Guard to Ituria, I will repeat your message to the birds and tell them to meet you at the large rock," Jan whispered. "You and Megan, please be careful!"

"Thanks, Jan," Knocker answered, then looking at Megan, "Megan, are you ready?"

"I am ready," Megan replied. She was now steady on her feet, able to walk, and possibly run if needed while still in her human form.

"Jan, wait at the cave entrance," Knocker instructed. "Make sure you are not seen. Once the poachers run away, go to where they are now—you can see them to the left, which is where the eggs are being stolen. Do you see them?"

"Yes, I can see them," Jan whispered, hiding behind the cave entrance, just barely peering outside.

"Okay, let's go!" Knocker called to Megan. "We'll see you soon, Jan. You be careful, too!"

Crouching behind the rock inside the cave entrance, Jan watched as Knocker and Megan left, heading right toward the poachers.

Chapter Twelve

FOLLOW THE LEADER

As Knocker and Megan grew closer to the poachers, they started yelling. However, to Jan, it sounded like angry, growling dogs! This loud growling mixed with the hundreds of birds screeching at the humans. *I wonder if Knocker has a second translation stone or if the poachers only hear the growling?*

Some of the terns tried swooping into the midst of the poachers, trying to stop them and save their eggs. However, the poachers just swiped at them, paying no attention to their desperate efforts. As Knocker grew closer, Jan saw them look up to see who was yelling at them, then took off, running down the path, each carrying what looked like a bagful of eggs.

When the poachers were out of sight, it was Jan's turn. Checking once again to confirm there was no one left atop the cliff, she ran toward the left side where the eggs had been stolen. Terns circled her, and as she got closer, they swooped in, trying to attack her also.

"Wait, please listen!" Jan called out. "Knocker, First Guard to Ituria, has sent me to give you a message."

Amazingly, several of the terns close to her landed before her, looking up, waiting for her to speak further.

"Knocker and Megan will rescue your eggs. You must follow me if your eggs have been stolen. We need to meet them at the bottom of the cliff. Please follow me!"

"How can this human able to talk to us?" asked one tern, turning to look at another tern near him.

"Maybe she is part of Knocker's alliance, a non-human that just looks human," replied the second tern.

"Yes, I am with Knocker's Alliance, Ituria's Alliance to save animals. Please listen to me!" she repeated to the terns still circling overhead.

"We will listen. What does Knocker want us to do?" a third tern said as it landed. "We have just lost our eggs, our children. What can we do to save them?"

Jan repeated Knocker's words, "Knocker, First Guard to Ituria, will rescue your eggs, and take you and your eggs to a safe place. If your eggs are gone, you must follow me down the cliff. Please follow me, and we will reunite you with your eggs."

The terns in the area started circling, and one called out to Jan and said, "We will follow you. Knocker is our friend."

Flying in a larger circle above her head, another called to the other terns, "The evil Knocker warned us about has come to pass; our eggs are gone. Knocker says to follow this human, and he will reunite us with our eggs."

Following his lead, Jan continued calling out, "Knocker asks you to follow me. If your eggs have been taken, please follow me so we can get the eggs back to you. He is rescuing them now."

Jan started down the path, continuing to call out every minute or so, until a trail of terns flew behind her. She could hear them talking with each other, mostly in screeches, since the terns were flying above and behind her; many were more than ten feet. They would not understand her, but the word had gotten out that she was the one leading them to their stolen eggs.

The sun was still out, and as Knocker had mentioned, the moon was now visible in the sky. It was not a full moon. However, it was close enough to be bright tonight. Jan hoped all had gone well, that Knocker and Megan's mission was successful. Only a few hundred more feet until the rock, then she and the terns will wait for Knocker's return there.

As they made the last curve toward the large rock, Jan could see Knocker and Megan already waiting for them. Knocker was carefully holding his duffle bag, and it looked full. She ran to them, and the terns followed her, a long line of terns, all searching for their missing eggs.

"Jan, great job!" Knocker called out as she got closer. "Thank you for bringing the terns here." Turning to the terns flying around her, Knocker continued, "Greetings my friends. Please all gather close, we haven't much time!"

"Jan, it would be better for you if you stayed here on the island, so please be careful not to enter the inner circle of the vortex once I form it, okay?" Knocker asked. "Also, please hand over the vase and tree to Megan. She can carry it during our journey."

Jan removed her backpack and took out the vase and tree; they were unharmed. "Here you are, Megan," she said as she handed it to Megan. She then slipped her backpack on again.

"Thank you," Megan replied, a smile brightening her face. "I am glad to return it to its owner."

"I am glad you are on your way to a new home!" Jan responded, smiling back, then to Knocker, "I'm not sure what a vortex is, but I will stay away from you and Megan, keeping just close enough for the translation stone to let me communicate with you." Jan backed up a few steps, letting the remaining birds gather near Knocker.

"Megan, are you ready?" Knocker called over to her.

Since Megan was on the other side of the rock, her answer was in growls.

Looking at the moon, Knocker called out, "Guardian, we are ready!"

What happened next was so quick, Jan almost wasn't sure she could believe her eyes. Knocker turned into a dragon—a giant dragon with shiny blue-green scales and blue wings! He flapped his large wings together, and a blue shaft of light started to form, a pillar of blue light heading straight to the moon!

"What's going on? What is happening?" Jan called out.

"Jan!" Knocker called back to warn her. "Stay back, or you will be pulled into the vortex!"

Jan watched as several terns started to moving up into the blue stream of light—they were not flying! Something was pulling them skyward!

A moment later, growling and roaring came from Megan. Suddenly, Knocker turned and his dragon claw grabbed Jan, placing her into the blue vortex with the terns.

"Jan!" Knocker called out with sudden alarm. "You are not safe here. You must return with us!"

Jan looked behind her, and one of the poachers had returned, a knife in hand as he approached them.

"Guardian, now!" shouted Knocker.

Instantly, Jan felt herself being pulled off the ground, just like the terns had just a few moments ago. They were all flying in the air, rapidly heading skyward!

Chapter Thirteen

ITURIA'S ISLAND

"Jan, wake up," Knocker said, gently touching her shoulder. "We must return to the campsite before 7:30 p.m. when your father returns home."

Jan opened her eyes, trying to remember where she was and what was happening. The last thing she remembered was being lifted into the sky by a dragon. She must have been dreaming. "What happened?" she murmured as she woke. "Where are we?"

Looking around, she tried to gather her thoughts. She saw Knocker, and he was a human again. *Did I imagine him being a dragon?* However, Megan was a dragon again, and beside her stood a large white horse—with a horn sticking from its forehead? *Am I seeing things? Is that a unicorn?*

"Greetings, Jan of Earth," said the unicorn. "I am Ituria, and you are on my island under the surface of the moon. Thank you for your assistance in rescuing the terns and their eggs, and for rescuing Megan, who has agreed to live here and help care for our rescued animals."

Knocker reached down and helped Jan to her feet. "Sorry I had to wake you. Traveling through the vortex makes most humans fall asleep. However, we must return to the Earth before 7:30 p.m., or your father will beat us back to camp. It is already after five, so we must leave soon."

"I'm not sure what is going on, but whatever you need me to do, just let me know." From the corner of her eye, she saw a basket full of eggs and about forty terns sitting on the floor. The vase and tree were also there. The events of the past few hours were returning to her now. *Is this just a dream? Is this really happening?*

"Don't worry about the tree for now," Knocker noted as he saw her stare at it. "I will take that back to its island once we return you home!"

"Where will you take the terns?" Jan asked. "What will happen to them?"

Ituria stepped forward. "We have a cavern we call the Asian Coastline. We have sealed it off to allow for air and water to be present. We even stocked the water with plants and various sea creatures. There are also birds rescued from previous years to make it a working ecosystem." Walking over to the group of terns, he said to them, "There are several rocky islands resembling where you lived before. There is also enough room for you to remain here, to raise your children in peace, free from human intervention."

"We will be glad to stay here," said one of the terns. "Thank you for allowing Knocker and his allies to rescue us."

"I must tell you … the Asian Coastline contains the same perils the Earth coastline does, absent the human intervention." Ituria's voice grew serious. "We have rescued many creatures, and all have their place in the circle of life. You will need to be careful and protect your family, just as you did on Earth."

Looking over at the eggs, Jan asked, "How will you know which egg belongs to which tern? Is there a type of magic for that?"

"That is one matter we have not resolved yet." Walking over to the basket of eggs, Ituria noted, "we may be able to distinguish between the smaller Chinese Crested Tern eggs and the larger Greater Crested Terns. However, the individual eggs will never match with their natural parents."

"How will we know which children are ours?" one tern asked anxiously.

"How can we tell, is there no way?" demanded another. "I want my children. There has to be a way!"

"Unfortunately," Knocker explained, "the poachers mixed the eggs together. Their scents are mixed or have been wiped off, so there is no way we can separate them to distinguish which egg belongs to which parent."

"What can we do? How can we raise these babies if we don't know who they belong to?" questioned another tern.

"I have an idea," Jan said, walking toward the terns. "Each of you has been transported here to save your children. Since there is no way to determine which are yours, why not form a large family, and the children will belong to all of you?"

"But that's not the way we do it. We take care of our own children," replied the first tern. "We feed and protect only our children. That is how it has always been done."

"Where I live," Jan replied, "it takes a village to raise a child. Each of you can be responsible for one egg, to warm and hatch and feed the chick. Then as a flock, or village, each of you will help the others when you can. Watching out for the chicks, protecting them, and helping each other to ensure they are fed. You will need each other's support to survive this new land." Jan placed her hand gently on the basket of eggs. "This is the best way possible for everyone, especially your chicks. Each one of these chicks needs someone to love and care for them. Can you open your heart and love the chick that is given to you as your own?"

Chapter Fourteen

RETURNING TO EARTH

"I will raise the one that is chosen for me," said the first tern, realizing the importance of Jan's words. "I will raise him or her as my own, and we will form a family."

"I agree," said another. "Let's be off to our new home and start our nests!"

"Yes," agreed a third. "We will raise them together, making sure each of them grows big and strong!"

"Thank you, Jan, that is a good solution," said Ituria, then he turned to the terns. "Will each of you pledge to hatch one egg as your own, even if we can't identify the natural parents?" Ituria asked. "If so, Knocker can take you to your new homes so you can start your new lives together as soon as he gets Jan back to her home."

The terns nodded in agreement and gathered around the eggs, talking with each other, ready to start their new adventure.

"Ituria," Knocker said as he turned toward him. "Russ sends his greetings, and thanks you for rescuing these terns and their eggs. He said, even though the governments have started passing laws to protect these endangered terns, there are always those who break the law to make a profit, not caring about the damage they create."

"Please send Russ my greetings," Ituria replied, "and thank him once again for making sure those in peril are rescued. We are grateful for his assistance."

"Now," Ituria continued, turning to Jan, "we need to get you back to Earth before you are missed. Should Guardian send you to the same spot, is that safe?"

"No," Knocker answered, shaking his head. "The only reason I brought Jan through the vortex is because Megan saw a poacher returning, and he had a knife, so we could not leave her behind. Possibly Guardian can send us to the top of the cliff where the cave is, just outside the cave? That will allow us to survey the situation before others see us."

"Guardian!" called out Ituria to no one in particular. "Can you do this? Knocker can create the vortex to allow you to send him and Jan back."

A voice from out of the air replied, "Yes, that is possible. Please make sure only those going back to Earth enter the vortex!" The voice resonated in the cave, slightly echoing, then faded away. Jan thought it sounded like someone talking over a loudspeaker, but of course she couldn't see any speakers.

"I see you are a little perplexed," Ituria said. "Guardian is located northeast of here in another cavern, and he has the power to transport us back and forth to the Earth. Knocker, in his dragon form, creates the vortex, and those in the vortex are transported."

"We need to get you back to Earth and Knocker back here before 9:00 tonight, so let's get started," Ituria continued as he backed away. "Knocker, when you are ready!"

Knocker walked out into the clearing, motioning Jan to join him. "Please grab your backpack and stand in front of me. That way, you will be inside the vortex when it is formed."

"Okay," Jan said as she walked over. "This is still so strange. Is this really happening?"

"Yes, this is real," Knocker replied softly. "Russ and I, along with many others, are part of Ituria's Alliance, a secret group of humans and animals working together to rescue endangered animals. Since you are now aware of it, it will be your choice whether to join us or not. However, you must tell no one about the Alliance, as it would put us all in danger. Can we trust you to keep our secret?"

"I will keep your secret, I promise," Jan said. "I will not tell anyone."

"Also, I need you to return the translation stone to me now. As long as I hold it, if you stay near me, you will still understand me."

Jan pulled the stone out of her pocket and handed it to Knocker. "Here you go. I am still amazed this small stone allowed me to understand terns, dragons, and unicorns!"

"Goodbye to you, Ituria and Megan," she called out, waving. "I am glad we have met and wish you all the best!"

"Goodbye, Jan," Ituria responded. "Perhaps we will meet again. Take care!"

"Goodbye, Jan," Megan added. "You will be remembered as a good human!"

"Are you ready?" Knocker said.

"Ready as I'll ever be!" Jan replied, not sure what would happen next.

"Okay, just stay where you are, and we'll head back to Earth," Knocker said as he backed away just a little. Within seconds he had transformed back into a dragon, towering above her as he flapped his wings forward to form a blue light around them.

"Guardian, we are ready!" he shouted.

Jan felt herself being lifted into the air again, trying to stay focused on how this worked. However, within a few moments, she was fast asleep.

Chapter Fifteen

POACHERS ARE BACK AGAIN

"Jan, wake up," Knocker whispered as he touched her shoulder. "We are back on Earth. You must be quiet, though, as two of the poachers have returned."

Jan opened her eyes, once again trying to remember what was happening. She had fallen into a deep asleep again, even though she tried to stay awake. *It must be something to do with the vortex and how it works.*

Looking around, trying to get her bearings, she noticed she and Knocker were sitting just inside the cave atop the cliff. They were hidden by the shadows of the cave. As she looked out the opening, she could see two people further down on the cliff, moving about and swinging at terns as they circled and flew into them. The poachers were here for more eggs!

"What can we do now?" Jan asked Knocker.

"At this point, I need to protect you since one of them has a knife," Knocker replied as he moved closer to the cave entrance. "We can possibly scare them away, but we won't be able to rescue the eggs. It is almost dark, and your dad and Russ will be back soon. They are to return by 7:30 p.m., and it is almost seven now. I must return you to camp before my potion wears off," Knocker whispered. "I cannot take another immediately because it is unsafe. I have to wait a week before taking another potion. That is why I must be out of camp before nine."

"What if we go around the left side, where they already stole the eggs?" Jan suggested. "They may not see us until we get past them. Then, we can run the rest of the way."

"That may work," Knocker agreed, nodding his head. "Okay, let's stay to the left and stay low."

Knocker and Jan quietly left the cave, bending over in hopes that the poachers would not look up and see them. All was going well until one of the terns flying above the poachers looked their way.

Suddenly, it started screeching and flying directly toward Knocker and Jan, drawing attention to itself and to them. As it got within ten feet of Knocker, Jan could understand it's message.

"Please, Knocker, come help!" it called out. "They are stealing our eggs!"

All the commotion caused the closest poacher to look up in their direction.

One man shouted to the other one, pointing to Knocker, then waving for him to follow the first as he started running away.

No chance of getting down the cliff path unnoticed now. If the poachers left before them, they should be able to return to camp in time. But what could they do to help the terns get back their eggs?

Looking over the cliff to the mainland, Jan saw that the researcher's boat already crossing the channel. Maybe they could bluff the poachers into leaving the eggs?

"If you leave the eggs," Jan shouted at them, "we won't turn you in. The researchers are on their way back and will stop you if you have those eggs with you. Set them down, and you can get away!"

They looked at Jan, however, didn't seem to understand what she was saying. *She was speaking in English, and they didn't understand English!*

"Knocker," Jan said. "They probably don't speak English, so they don't know what I'm saying. Can you run up there with your translation stone and repeat the message? They understood you when you talked with them earlier, even though I only heard growls and roars."

"Don't get too close, though!" Jan added. "If you can get the eggs back then you can take them and their parents back with you when you go back to the moon."

"I will try," Knocker agreed. "You keep going down the path toward camp, and I'll go talk to them again, try to get them to leave the eggs. If I can get the eggs back, I will take you and the other parents that are missing eggs with me. You have to gather together and follow me, so I know who is missing their eggs. And make sure I can still see you at all times, okay? You may not understand me, but I can signal how things are going."

Jan nodded and headed down the path, veering left. Knocker took off running to the right after the two poachers. As soon as he was close enough, he repeated Jan's message, although Jan could only hear the growling.

"If you leave the eggs, you can leave the island without getting caught!" he called out. "The researchers are almost back, and they will not let you leave if you have the eggs with you."

Knocker was having to shout to them as they were running, having to keep within ten feet of them so his words would be translated into human speak, rather than dragon speak.

Suddenly, there was growling coming from the cave, Jan looked at the cave entrance— *Megan is back*!

Megan looked at Jan, then started running toward Knocker. Knocker bent down to pick up something and headed back toward Megan and Jan. Jan heard growling as they talked to each other, *what is going on?* She raced toward them, knowing if she got close enough, she would understand them.

As she watched the poachers jump onto a small boat, she reached Megan. "What's going on? Why are you back?" She hoped Megan would understand.

"There is one more critical step to this mission, and Knocker cannot do it," Megan answered.

Knocker ran up, showing the small bag of eggs the poachers left as they ran to their boats. "Russ and the others are in the harbor now. The poachers dropped these eggs and jumped on their boat. Hopefully, they are gone for today. Why are you back, Megan?"

Chapter Sixteen

KNOCKER DEPARTS

"**S**ome of the mates of the birds we took to the moon were out searching for food and will be returning around dark tonight," Megan explained.

Jan was trying to follow the conversation and was sure someone had a translation stone at this point—she didn't but she could still understand Knocker and Megan.

Megan continued, "I need to stay until tomorrow to make sure everyone in the tern families is reunited. I have been assigned by Ituria to be the dragon guardian for the terns while they get used to their new home, and we need to find their mates if possible, so I'm here until tomorrow."

Looking at Knocker, she said, "You will need to go back now, take those eggs and the terns you have gathered. I will return tomorrow with the other terns."

"Megan, thank you again," Knocker replied with appreciation for her help. "I will meet with you tomorrow. Are you good with the transport protocols?"

"Yes." Megan nodded. "Ituria and Guardian explained them to me." Her voice grew worried as they contemplated all that needed to happen in just a few minutes. "You must go now! Jan and I will head back to camp. I have a translation stone and will stay with her."

"We have to return soon," Jan agreed. "They will arrive at camp in a few minutes, and we must be there when they do."

Knocker turned to Jan. "Thank you for all your help. I will return to the moon, and Megan has noted that she will remain until tomorrow morning. Please stay with Megan, as she will not be familiar with the camp or how to deal with humans."

"I will, Knocker," Jan replied. "Please be safe and thank you for solving my mystery!"

Turning to Megan as she started down the path, Jan said, "Come on, we need to beat them to camp!"

"One minute," Megan replied. "I need to talk to the birds."

Megan ran into the middle of the birds and started growling at them, and they were answering back, some nodding their heads. Once done, Megan ran back to Jan.

"Okay, good to go!" Megan said. "I told them to tell anyone who was missing their eggs or their mate to meet us here tomorrow morning, and we will get them back together."

"Good thinking!" Jan noted. "That will save you time in the morning looking for them. They will be waiting here for you."

They both stopped and looked back for a few seconds as Knocker called out to the terns to join him, transformed into an impressive dragon, formed the blue light vortex, and all were transported to the moon. While it took less than minute, it was a mesmerizing sight! Then they started down the path again, hoping to beat the research boat.

It took about ten minutes for Jan and Megan to reach camp, arriving just as the boat was pulling into the dock.

"We made it!" she whispered to Megan. "Let me explain why you are here in a way that will be acceptable to the researchers. I will introduce you as Knocker's cousin, and you came to help out and complete his research project." Jan was focusing on telling a rational story that everyone would believe. Even though Knocker said he and Mr. Russell were friends, she was not sure how much Mr. Russell knew or if she should reveal who Megan really was.

Megan nodded. She was not sure how to react to humans, so would let Jan lead the way in any conversations involving them.

As the boat party got closer, Jan waved and said, "Hi! Welcome back!"

"Hey, Jan," called out her dad. "We made back it before dark! Can you help carry supplies?"

"Of course!" she answered as they walked toward the boat that was now tied to the dock. "We'll be there in just a minute!" Jan motioned for Megan to follow her, and they went to help carry the supplies back to the food tent.

"We got some fresh bread, Jan!" her dad called out as he put the supplies on the dock.

"Sounds good!" she replied as she picked up two bags and handed them to Megan, then grabbed a large box and started back to camp.

"Megan," Jan whispered. "Just stay with me. I'll make some quick introductions and then I'll take you to Knocker's tent to relax. You have had a busy day!"

"Thank you, Jan," Megan replied. "I would like to relax for a bit before returning to the cliff in the morning."

George and Russell followed Jan and Megan into the supply tent, everyone carrying bags and boxes and placing them on an open table.

"Dad and Mr. Russell," Jan started. "I want to introduce you to Megan, who is Knocker's cousin. Knocker had to leave a few minutes before you returned, but Megan has agreed to stay and finish up Knocker's research notes, and then head home tomorrow after lunch when her ride returns."

George smiled at Megan. "Nice to meet you, Megan!"

Megan nodded back and said, "Thanks, I'm glad to help out Knocker."

George turned to the bags of food and started putting away supplies in the cabinets.

Russ looked at Megan for a few seconds before speaking, then said, "Yes, nice to meet you. Any friend of Knocker's is a friend of mine. Welcome to camp!"

Megan replied, "Thank you for the welcome. Knocker said his research is almost done and only a few more items to be completed. I should be done by tomorrow."

"Okay," Jan said. "I'm going to take Megan to Knocker's tent to get a little rest before dinner. Glad everyone made it back safe!"

Jan turned to leave, waving for Megan to join her. "Come this way, Megan," she said. "I'll show you where you can rest for a bit."

Knocker's tent was a few tents down from the supply tent, and was about twelve feet square inside, just enough room for a bed, a desk, and some shelves to hold clothes and papers.

"You can rest here for a while," Jan started in a loud voice, then continued in a soft voice, whispering as she lowered the tent flap, "Great job! No one was suspicious. We can just keep you separated until tomorrow morning and then you can be back on your way."

Megan nodded her head in agreement and smiled. But her smile quickly disappeared as she looked behind Jan, watching the tent flap lift.

Chapter Seventeen

SECRETS REVEALED

"**T**his is where you will stay tonight," Jan said to Megan as Russ followed them into the tent. "You have a bed here to sleep." She pointed at the bed in the left corner. "This is where Knocker's research papers are." She then pointed to a small desk with several folders and notebooks piled on top. "Let's meet after dinner to go through them and finalize them."

"Thanks, Jan," Megan replied cautiously, glancing at Russ. "I would appreciate your help getting this all together. I'll need to get everything ready to meet back up with Knocker tomorrow."

Russ walked over to the table where the two girls were talking and reviewing documents. He looked at the documents for a minute, then looked at Megan. *How is she related to Knocker? Does she know? She must if she is meeting him again tomorrow. I must be sure, though, before revealing anything of our mission.*

"So, tell me, Megan," he started, "Jan says you are a cousin of Knocker's. Have you worked on research with him before?"

"Actually, no," Megan replied with a little hesitation. "We met just recently, and he told me of how he worked with endangered animals, and I volunteered to help when I could." *Knocker said Russ knows; does he know everything? How can I be sure? Can I trust this human as I trust Jan? I cannot reveal myself without knowing for sure.*

Jan looked at Russ and Megan, seeing that each was wary of the other. There was no trust yet, that would have to be earned. *What can I do to break through the walls of suspicion? Neither will speak the truth to the other without more information. What common factor other than Knocker is there?*

There was an awkward silence in the room. Megan began picking up and shuffling papers but not actually reading them. Russ stood a few feet back, wondering what he could say and not say.

Jan had a thought on what could break the tension.

"Mr. Russell," Jan said as she turned to look at him. "Knocker says you know a friend of his, someone named Ituria. How did you meet?" She hoped this would draw Russ into a meaningful dialogue that Megan could relate to, the common connection was Ituria!

Now Russ looked a Jan with a puzzled face. *Does she know too? How much does she know?*

"Yes," he answered cautiously. "I do know Ituria. We met many years ago and are still good friends." *What else should I say? I cannot reveal our secret unless I know for sure they are both part of Ituria's Alliance.*

"We saw Ituria this afternoon when Megan was dropped off here to help Knocker, and Ituria wishes you his best and thanks you for your help on this research."

That should open the doors of communication, Jan hoped.

"You saw him this afternoon?" asked Russ. *How could they have seen Ituria?*

"Yes, we both saw him today. He is well and is glad that Knocker, and now Megan, can help with your current research project." Jan was hoping she would get the right answers to this statement. If not, she would not reveal anything further.

Seeing where Jan was going with the conversation, Megan added, "Yes, we both talked with him, and Ituria asked me to help with the terns while Knocker goes to his next assignment."

Russ looked at both girls for a few moments, thinking about what they had just revealed. Then he responded, almost in a whisper. "If you met with Ituria, then you know our mission. No one else in this research camp is aware, so it must remain a secret between us alone. Please tell me what happened this afternoon; is Knocker okay?"

It was Megan who responded, "Yes, he is well. He could not leave Ituria's Island, so I need to complete his mission." Megan looked closely at Russ, knowing that he had earned Knocker's trust. *Could she trust him also?*

"Good news!" Russ replied. "I am so relieved he is okay." His face relaxed, and he smiled for just a moment, then added, "Knocker and I have known each other for many years, and we have gone on many missions together." Russ became serious again as he whispered, "Please tell me what is left to accomplish on Knocker's mission."

Megan looked at Jan, her eyes widened and there was a concerned look on her face. *I'm still not sure I can trust this human.* Seeing Megan's hesitancy, Jan wanted Russ to reveal more information.

"Have you been to Ituria's Island?" Jan asked as she looked at Russ. She wanted to know just how much more they could reveal, how much he really knows.

"Yes," Russ replied. "That was my first encounter with Ituria and Knocker. A beautiful place! I am glad that Ituria started his Islands so many years ago, and I am always glad to help when they need human assistance!"

That was what Megan needed to hear. *He knows Knocker is not human.* "Thank you, Russ. Although I am new to this, I will work with you two humans to complete Knocker's mission. Only you two know my true form, and that I have been given a translation stone to hold so I can communicate with you."

Chapter Eighteen

FINAL PLANS

Russ nodded with understanding as he took in this new information, then bowed to Megan, realizing that she was also a dragon and deserved his respect. "Thank you, Megan. We are glad to have your assistance. Please let us know what final steps are needed to complete Knocker's mission."

Bowing to Russ to acknowledge her trust in him, Megan answered softly so no others would hear. She knew that if anyone heard her from outside the tent, they would hear a dragon. "Knocker has retrieved the stolen eggs from the poachers and taken them to Ituria's Island, along with many of the parents. However, some parents were out searching for food, so were not part of the group transported today. My mission, as given by Ituria, is to gather the remaining terns together that are missing their eggs and partners and return tomorrow bringing them back to rejoin their families."

Explaining further their plan, Jan added, "Megan will sit on the cliff at site three where the eggs were stolen for a few hours tomorrow morning, then Guardian will transport her and the terns back to Ituria. She talked with the terns still on the cliff, asking them to relay the message for anyone missing their eggs or mates to stay on the cliff and wait for Megan's return in the morning."

"I understand," Russ acknowledged. "Will you need anything further from me at this point other than to keep the other researchers off of site three?"

"I don't think so, Mr. Russell," Jan replied. "If Megan and I are on the cliff in the morning, we can gather everyone together."

"Jan," Russ answered, "if you are going with Megan in the morning, I would like to meet you at site three once the transport occurs; you should not be alone up there or walking back to camp. Is that okay? As Knocker told your dad earlier, the poachers have been to the cliff before and know there are more eggs to be stolen."

"I should be safe as long as Megan is there," Jan replied, looking at Megan with a smile. Looking back at Russ, she continued, "What if you meet me at site three at noon? Does that work into your schedule?"

"I will do whatever is needed to help Megan complete her task," Russ said. "I would suggest you two eat dinner in this tent, as the translation stone has a limited range, and we don't want anyone outside of its range hearing Megan's natural voice."

"Jan, your dad found you some fresh bread, so I can bring that, cheese, and fruit, as I know you don't eat meat. Does that sound good?" Russ asked.

"That will be fine, thank you!" Jan replied. "I am hungry. It has been a long day."

Russ looked at Megan, thinking of what they had to offer her. "What do you prefer, Megan?

Knocker usually joined Jan in her vegetarian meals, but I will do my best to provide you with whatever you find appetizing for dinner. We just came back with many supplies, so would have fish or meat if that is your preference."

Megan looked at Jan, thinking of what options were available, then back at Russ. "I will share whatever Jan is having, thank you." Megan looked at Jan with a smile. She had been eating only mushrooms for over 300 years, so anything besides mushrooms would be a feast!

Jan nodded in agreement. "Mr. Russell, thank you for offering to bring the food back to us. I don't want to leave Megan alone at this point, until she gets used to her surroundings."

Russ left the tent and returned in a few minutes, with two plates full of bread, cheese, apples, and grapes. He brought two bottles of water also, to go with the meal.

"Here you are ladies!" he called out as he entered. "I hope you enjoy your dinner."

"Thank you so much, Mr. Russell!" Jan exclaimed. "This looks great!"

"My thanks also," Megan added. "I will certainly enjoy this!"

"You are both welcome!" Russ replied, smiling as he handed them the plates. Getting a little closer, he whispered to them. "Please do not leave before sunlight tomorrow morning. I will be up and will make sure you reach site three without difficulty. Then I will leave you and return at noon, since Jan indicates that all will be done by then. Are we all agreed?"

Jan and Megan looked at each other, thinking through Russ's statements, and both nodded to Russ.

"Jan, I also have a cot outside I can move in here so you can stay with Megan tonight. It would probably be best if you stayed together until morning."

"I agree, that's a great idea! Thank you, Mr. Russell," Jan responded. She held the tent flap while he moved the cot inside, so she and Megan could stay in the same tent overnight.

"Sleep well, and we will meet in the morning!" Russ called out as he left.

Chapter Nineteen

MORNING BREAKS

Jan turned to Megan, as they each held a plate of food. "Why don't we eat first, and then you can rest. Even a dragon would need a rest after the long day you've had."

"I agree," Megan replied. "I am tired and hungry. I guess I need to get used to acting like a human, and this will taste so different than the mushrooms. I am looking forward to dinner!"

After a few minutes of silence while both girls ate, Megan smiled at Jan. "I am glad that you and Knocker found me. No matter what happens, I will remember you with gratitude."

"I am glad you are no longer trapped," Jan replied, smiling back. "Unless you have any questions, we need to sleep early, so we can rise at dawn. It has been a while since you have seen the sun rise, and I thought you might want to see it in the morning."

"What a great idea!" Megan responded with enthusiasm. "I would so much like to see the sun rise in the morning. As you said, it has been a long time."

Looking over to the desk, Megan continued, "Do we need to do anything with Knocker's papers?

I can't read them, so I would need you to help get them together."

"No, don't worry about those. Mr. Russell and I will handle them tomorrow. Mr. Russell always handled Knocker's paperwork, and now I know why!" Jan smiled.

"Let's rest now, I'll stay on the cot near the door, so no one walks in looking for Knocker and finds you," Jan continued. "Everyone on our main team knew he was leaving today, but I just want to be sure you are safe. Please lay on the bed and see if you can get comfortable. I hope it is better than the rocks you have been laying on."

Megan laid on the bed, stretching her legs a bit before settling in. "This is so comfortable!" she exclaimed. "Definitely better than the hard rock floor of the cave."

Jan thought that all the excitement of the day would keep her awake late into the night; however, she was asleep in a few minutes.

Waking up the next morning, it was still dark, but the glow of the horizon to the east showed Jan the sun would be up shortly. She looked over to Megan's bed, but she wasn't there. *Where could she be?*

Jumping up and heading out of the tent, she looked around camp. Toward the harbor side, she saw Megan in her human form, standing and facing the harbor. The pre-dawn rays of the sun were announcing that the sunrise would break very soon.

"I'm glad I found you," Jan said softly as she got closer to Megan. "How long have you been up?"

"There were so many noises, I couldn't sleep," Megan started. "I saw you fall asleep and listened for a while. My curiosity got the best of me, and I snuck out a little while ago, trying to identify the many sounds—the waves hitting the dock, boats bumping against poles, local birds and wildlife talking."

"It has been a long time since you last heard these sounds. I'm glad you could experience them again," Jan said, appreciating that to Megan this was all so different. "There is so much that you can do, and I hope your life on Ituria's Island with the terns will be enjoyable."

"I am looking forward to it," Megan said. Turning to the east, she stared at the horizon. "It has been so long since I have seen a sunrise."

Both girls watched in silent admiration as the first rays of the sun broke the surface of the horizon over the water and sunlight started streaming over the land.

After a few minutes, Megan turned to Jan. "You do need to know, though, that the small boat down there arrived a little while ago, and three people jumped off and headed up the path."

Jan looked down at the boat, it looked the same as the one she remembered leaving yesterday, *could they be the same?* If they are the same poachers from yesterday, waiting at the top of the cliff for the terns is not going to go smoothly.

"Did they look like the people from yesterday?" Jan asked.

"They were dressed the same, just a pair of pants and shirt, all similarly dressed, just like yesterday.

Dark clothes, so they would not stand out in the darkness. I'm used to the dark, so saw them jump off. They were trying to hide from view, and quickly went from the boat to the side of the cliff."

"We can't take the chance of them being the same, we will need to work with Mr. Russell to change our plans," Jan decided. "We can meet the terns somewhere else, and we just need to get the message to them."

Megan nodded. "Perhaps some of the other terns from other cliffs can help us get the word to the top cliff. That way we won't have to go there."

"Good idea!" Jan exclaimed. "You will be able to talk with the terns on the other cliffs, and they should help us!"

Suddenly, Jan realized that at least one of the poachers saw Knocker as a dragon and saw them all transported to Ituria's Island. *What if he is back seeking the dragon?*

"Megan," she whispered. "One of them saw Knocker as a dragon. What if they are looking for a dragon? We can't let them see you as a dragon! Is there another way to get the terns to Ituria's Island?"

Chapter Twenty

CHANGE OF PLANS

"Good morning, ladies, you are up early!" said Russ cheerfully as he walked up to Jan and Megan. The worried look on their faces changed his mood quickly, and he asked, "What's wrong?"

"Good morning, Mr. Russell," Jan said. "Megan saw three poachers come to the island on that boat early this morning and head to the cliffs. We will need to change our plans!"

Megan added, "I cannot leave until about noon, when there is a direct line from the moon to our position. Guardian explained that he can only transport in a straight line and the moon will be visible during the day today; however, not until about noon. I cannot leave until then."

"Also, Mr. Russell," Jan said, "you need to know that Megan has not been around humans for over three hundred years, so we will need to assist her in dealing with them."

Jan looked at Megan, and Megan nodded her head. That was all she wanted to reveal about her past.

"There are several things to consider at this point," Jan continued, "At least one of the poachers saw Knocker turn into a dragon and transport Megan, myself, and numerous birds through the blue vortex. I can only think that they are back to find the dragon who lives on this island." Russ nodded and waited for her to continue.

"Second, they are most likely waiting for us on site three, as that was where they stole the eggs and where Knocker and Megan appeared and made them return the eggs."

"Then you cannot go to site three at this time," Russ said immediately. "I will have to find a way I can go there and get the birds to join you somewhere else."

Russ reached into his pocket and pulled out a notebook. Inside was a drawing of the island they were on, with several circled numbers appearing on top.

Pointing to the circled three, he said, "This is where you were yesterday and were planning to go today." Pointing down and a little to the left, he continued, "Here is site four, a little lower down but not visible from site three. This should be your new meeting place for the terns. The poachers will not see you if you stay here."

"It looks like we take the path to site three about half-way, and then turn to the left," Jan said, her finger

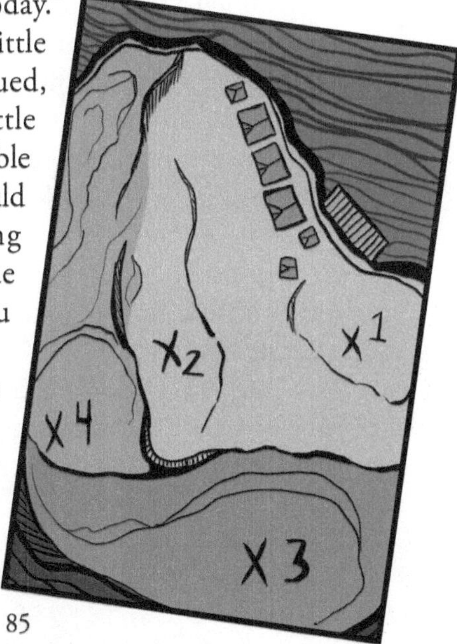

following along with the path on the map. "Is that correct?"

"Yes," Russ said. "Why don't you and Megan wait at site four, and I'll go to the edge of site three, and call for the terns. I'll need to borrow your translation stone, Megan. Will that be acceptable, so I can talk with the terns?"

"I promised Ituria I would bring it back with me, so I will trust you with it, as long as I get it back before I have to leave."

"I agree and promise to return it to you," Russ said. "When the terns get close enough to understand me, I will tell them where to meet you. If I get you to site four around ten o'clock while I head to site three, I'll get there by ten thirty. Then I can direct them to you."

"One point you both need to understand," Russ continued. "Without the translation stone, you won't be able to understand each other if you try to talk. That will make things a little difficult."

Megan and Jan nodded, then looked at each other.

"We can probably point and even draw pictures in the sand if needed for the short time when you are on site three," Jan replied.

"Okay, then. Let's grab some breakfast and get on with our mission!" Russ added, then turned to the supply tent.

"Megan," Jan said. "I usually have cheese and fruit for breakfast. I will pick something out for both of us and we can eat in Knocker's tent before we leave."

"Thanks, Jan." Megan smiled and replied, "I enjoyed dinner last night, so I'm sure this meal will be just as good."

Per the plan, Jan and Megan had breakfast, then Russ met them to walk up to site four, where they would stay until Russ could relay the message to the birds on site three.

"Please take care of this stone," Megan said as she handed it to Russ. "I have promised Ituria that I would return it to him."

"I understand, Megan," Russ said. "I will make sure you get this back before you leave. Please stay here on site four, and I will send the birds down to you. Site four is very isolated, so you should be able to create the vortex as soon as the moon is in view later today."

"Thank you, Russ, your help is greatly appreciated," Megan answered.

Russ turned and headed up the path toward site three and quickly disappeared from the girls' view. They sat together and looked out over the water, unable to talk but still admiring the sea's beauty.

Jan looked at her watch, and her eyes widened, it was almost 11:00. *Russ should have been to site three over half an hour ago, yet no terns have come to join Megan here on site four.*

Jan turned to Megan, then pointed at her watch. *How can she relay her worries that something was wrong?* She pointed to the birds, then pointed to the path, and back at her watch. Her mind was drawing a blank on how to explain her fear without words.

Then she saw a tern heading right for Megan, and it was screeching at her. Megan jumped up, growled to the tern, and started running, waving at Jan to follow her.

Something is wrong, but I don't know what! Megan must know. Jan ran after Megan and they both hurried up the path to site three, Jan not knowing what they would find there. Jan got to site three just a few seconds after Megan, however there was no one to be seen. Neither Russ nor the poachers were there! Jan looked at Megan and held out her hands and shrugged—trying to convey she did not know what was going on.

Megan turned to the terns flying around, and they were carrying on a conversation. Jan looked around, trying to see what they could be talking about, and saw the cave. *Could the poachers have taken Russ to the cave?* Jan tapped Megan on the shoulder and pointed in the direction of the cave.

Suddenly, a voice called out from the cave, "Don't come in. It's a trap!"

Chapter Twenty-One

SITE THREE

Jan recognized the voice as Russ's voice, *the poachers must be holding him captive in the cave!* Megan was talking to the terns and had come to the same conclusion. Jan and Megan looked at each other and nodded; they were going into the cave. There was a pile of tools and a rope dropped haphazardly in front of the opening, most likely belonging to the poachers.

Pulling a flashlight from her backpack, Jan pointed it into the cave, and moved forward. She and Megan watched carefully as they heard shuffling and saw movement in the back of the cave. Megan would have to get within ten feet of Russ to activate the translation stone so she could talk to the poachers.

The poachers start shouting at them, but neither Jan nor Megan understood what they were saying at this point. Jan could see Russ standing beside one of the poachers. The poacher was tightly holding onto Russ's arm.

Megan slowly approached down the middle of the cave, while Jan started down the left side. Once they got within ten feet of Russ, Megan started talking to them.

"Please let me know why you are here and what you want!" she called out.

Russ and Jan could understand, and so could the poachers. The one appearing to be the leader stepped closer and shouted at Megan. Unfortunately, the translation stone did not translate human languages, so neither Russ nor Jan knew what was being said.

Megan replied quickly, anger filling her voice, "My friend must remain unharmed, or you all will die!"

Jan and Russ looked at Megan, then at each other. The poachers' attention was on Megan as they started yelling back at her.

Jan had an idea and started slowly walking toward the left side of the cave, keeping her flashlight on Russ, and glanced at Megan, hoping Megan would understand her plan. *If I can get close enough to Russ, I can grab him and get down the left stairs.*

Megan gave Jan a quick glance and nodded, understanding that Jan was going to try and reach Russ. She would keep the poachers occupied so they would not notice.

Megan called back to the poachers, "As you saw yesterday, the dragon has left the island and will not return. Your presence has required that he leave. Humans and dragons cannot live in the same place!"

Two of the poachers started toward Megan, yelling again. Only the one holding Russ was staying near the back; however, he was distracted by the discussion taking place and it looked like his grip on Russ was not as tight as before.

"You take eggs from the terns!" Megan yelled back. "You are stealing their babies! We are here to help them and to stop you from taking their babies!"

With that, the third poacher joined the other two, ready to fight. Jan took the opportunity and grabbed Russ's hand and ran back toward the left staircase.

Before she got too far away, Jan yelled, "Do what you must do to be safe, Megan!"

"They're heading your way!" Megan called back.

"Mr. Russell, duck your head down, we have to go down these stairs now and it is very low!" Jan whispered quickly. She used her flashlight to show the steps, then the walls, back and forth, so they could get down quickly.

Once they made it down the stairs, Jan reached down and found several stones and rolled them across the floor, making it sound like she and Russ were running through the cave.

"Make no sound and stay against the wall!" Jan whispered urgently to Russ.

Throwing another handful of stones, Jan then backed with Russ into the corner in the darkness behind some rocks where they could not be seen from the stairs. They could hear footsteps. Jan turned off the flashlight and complete darkness enveloped them.

Two small shafts of light could be seen shining about as two of the poachers headed down the narrow stairway. They were talking with each other and headed toward the room at the end of the stairway, grumbling as they banged the heads into the stair walls, and tripping when they missed the steps.

Jan and Russ could hear their footsteps as the poachers ran past the rock that hid them. The first poacher pointed his flashlight across the cave and said something, then started running across, followed by the second.

Cracking sounds and screams filled the air as both poachers crashed through the animal claw tiles and fell into the pit below. Now the poachers were crying out in fear. They were alive but trapped!

Jan grabbed Russ's hand, turned on the flashlight and headed back up the left stairway. As soon as they got close to the top, Jan turned off her flashlight and waited for her eyes to adjust to the dim light of the cave. As the cries of the two trapped poachers echoed throughout the top cavern, Jan and Russ continued moving quietly toward the front of the cave where the remaining poacher and Megan were standing.

As soon as she saw Russ, Megan started speaking again, knowing that the translation stone would allow her to communicate.

"Your friends are trapped; can't you hear them?" Megan paused so all could hear the trapped poachers' cries.

She then continued with a command, "If you want to save them, you must do so now before the tide, as they will not survive the high tide."

Megan then waved for Jan and Russ to get behind her.

Jan and Russ quickly went to the front of the cave and stood behind Megan. Jan turned her flashlight to show the remaining poacher in the cave.

"Russ, I saw a rope outside the cave. They must have brought it here. Please bring it in and give it to this one," Megan called out to Russ.

Once Russ returned with the rope, Megan continued speaking, "Russ, please throw this one the rope, making sure to stay out of his reach." Russ walked a little closer to the poacher and threw the rope at his feet.

"Now, we will show you more mercy than you have shown us—here is a rope—rescue your friends before they drown. Then leave and never return to this island!" Megan's orders were clear, her voice left no doubt that she expected him to do what she said.

However, this guy wasn't going to let a little girl tell him what to do. He yelled something and started to approach Megan, waving his knife, trying to scare her into backing down.

Chapter Twenty-Two

FINAL RESOLUTION

"**E**nough!" Megan roared. She was done dealing with this human. Her voice echoed throughout the cave with the strength of a mighty dragon, not a young girl.

Jan looked at Megan, knowing she had to remain calm or she would turn back into a dragon, *just what the remaining poacher in the cave is searching for.*

"Megan," she whispered urgently, "you must remain calm, remember?"

Megan looked at Jan and slowly nodded, took a deep breath, then turned back to the poacher. In a strong but calmer voice she stated, "You have only one chance, and if you do not take it, we will seal you in this cave with your fellow thieves."

Emotion returned to her voice as she continued, "Do not underestimate my power or resolve!" The last sentence reverberated through the cave, driving home that she was done trying to reason with this human.

The poacher's eyes widened and his jaw dropped. He would not challenge her again. Grabbing the rope and turning on his flashlight, he hurried down the staircase to rescue the two trapped below.

As they emerged from the cave, Jan looked to the east and said to Megan, "Megan, the moon is now visible. You must leave before they get out of the cave."

"Agreed, and you must leave and go back to the camp now, since they have seen you. This is now a dangerous site." Turning to Russ, "Russ, I would advise you to not allow anyone to come up here. Please mark this site off limits."

"I agree, we will keep everyone on our team off this site," Russ said, nodding.

Turning toward the terns on the cliff, Megan called out to them. "Please join me now, as I must leave. If you have eggs missing, or your mates are missing, please come now!"

Looking at Russ, Megan said, "Russ, if you will give me Ituria's translation stone, I will return now to Ituria's Island with the remaining terns."

Russ reached in his pocket and pulled out the stone, handing it to Megan. She placed it in her pocket, and turned to Jan.

"Jan, you have my eternal gratitude and my best wishes." Megan then bowed gracefully to Jan.

"Thank you for your help and friendship, Megan," Jan replied, bowing back to her. "Please be safe in your new home!"

Megan said, "Both of you, please be safe. You must return to camp as soon as possible."

Turning her head to the moon rising above the horizon in the eastern sky, Megan shouted out, "Guardian, we are ready! Look for the blue vortex!"

Almost immediately, Megan transformed into an exquisite ruby-colored dragon with large grey wings, the sunshine shimmering over her large slender dragon body. Quickly, the terns waiting on the ground cried out and flew over to her.

She waved her large wings forward, creating a blue vortex and called to all the terns, "Please, get inside the blue light quickly!"

"Guardian, now!" she shouted, and she and the terns were drawn out of sight in a matter of seconds.

Russ and Jan stood and watched in silence as the transport to the moon took place.

Russ spoke first. "No matter how many times I see it, it is amazing how they can travel back and forth to the moon!"

"How long have you been doing this?" Jan said. "How long have you known Knocker and Ituria?"

"I would say for at least fifty years. I met them when I was a young teenager, about your age," Russ answered, remembering the first time he met them. "I have this to remind me that this is real, otherwise I would sometimes think I was dreaming. I keep it with me all the time."

Russ reached into his pocket and pulled out a shiny blue-green scale. "It's one of Knocker's scales. A reminder of my first trip to Ituria's Island." He smiled as he put the scale back in his pocket and added, "Jan, I'm glad that we have a new human recruit for Ituria's Alliance."

Jan replied with excitement, "Yes, I'm glad to be a part of this effort by Ituria."

She reached into her pocket and pulled out the little figure and showed it to Russ. "This will remind me that this really happened, and that Megan was a dragon that Knocker and I rescued."

"Well, we better return to camp now and gather all of Knocker and Megan's completed paperwork," said Russ with a wink. "Then we can discuss how you came to find Megan."

Jan winked and smiled back. "Yes, we'll need to finish it up before tomorrow." Jan thought for a moment, then continued, "We need to tell my dad the poachers stole some of the eggs since Knocker couldn't stop them because he was protecting me. That will explain the missing terns and eggs from the reports. We should also say that Megan was able to complete Knocker's work, so she went back home. Per Megan's suggestion, it is important to mark site three as off-limits."

"Agreed!" Russ replied. "I will also make sure that no one goes alone to any of the remaining sites, as we do not know if the poachers will return. I think that covers all the loose ends on this mission. If you think of anything else, please let me know."

"I will, Mr. Russell, and thanks for helping out!" Jan said as she smiled, remembering that in the last twenty-four hours she had helped to free Megan, rescue many tern eggs, and transport the eggs and their parents to Ituria's Island.

"You are welcome, I was glad to help. I have a lot of exciting stories to tell those who have been to Ituria's Island!" replied Russ.

"I can't wait to hear them! I hope you will include me in your missions in the future, rescuing animals and having Knocker transport them to Ituria's Island to be safe," Jan said. "What a great thing to do! I'll be glad to help Ituria's Alliance."

As Jan and Russ headed back to camp, they discussed how Russ first met Ituria and the many rescue missions that had taken place over the years as well as the missions that were still ahead.

THE END

Or is it?
Don't miss *Jan and the Search for Lilya!*

Note From The Author

While this story is a fantasy fiction novel, it is based on events that occurred several years ago before laws were enforced to protect wild tern eggs from being poached by local villagers. Although it was illegal, there was no reason for the villagers not to steal the wild seabird eggs, including eggs belonging to the rare Chinese Crested Tern. No governmental agency enforced the law, so it was ignored, and stolen eggs were sold to local restaurants. At this point in time, the forestry bureau covered land birds and the oceanography bureau covered only marine life living in the water. Protection of the Chinese Crested Tern fell into a regulatory loophole—there was a law to protect them, but no one oversaw enforcing it.

After it was realized that these terns had returned from extinction only to be threatened once again, the Xiangshan government and Zhejiang Museum of National History got together and created policies to protect seabirds, including better monitoring and public advertising that it was a crime to steal wild seabird eggs. After a few fishermen were arrested for doing so, the situation started to improve. With more work done by researchers and government officials, the Chinese Crested Tern now draws attention from many bird watchers who travel miles hoping to see one of these "birds of legend," so called because of their return after being declared extinct.

<u>Audubon Magazine</u>, Winter 2019, *A Legend Among the Masses*, Jane Qiu, author <u>https://www.audubon.org/magazine/winter-2019/inside-race-save-chinas-mysterious-bird-legend</u>

ABOUT THE AUTHOR

J.B. moved to Florida in her early teens and has lived there ever since, enjoying the mild weather and abundance of wildlife. She even spent several seasons raising orphan squirrels. She graduated from the University of Central Florida and has spent her working career in the legal profession. Her novels are inspired by her family and nature, as well as her need to escape from the real world once in a while.
www.facebook.com/J.B.Moonstar

Instagram @J.B.Moonstar

Twitter @jb_moonstar

jbmoonstar.author@gmail.com

website – jbmoonstar.com

Discover More by JB Moonstar

Chronicles of Ituria

Russ and The Hidden Voice

Taylor and the Red Wolf Rescue

Jenna and the Legend of the White Wolf

Jenna and the Eyes of Fire

Jan and the Secret Cave

Jan and the Search for Lilya

Taylor and the Final Nine

Michelle and the Missing Manatee

Jenna and the Broken Promise

Sara and the Secret Mission

& More Adventures to Come!

The Mermaids of Crystal Cay

Kimmi and the Sea Dragon

Roselia and the Ancient Warriors

& More Adventures to Come!

Coloring Book from

Artist Jenn Kotick

Mermaids

Book Club Questions

1. Why do many sea birds build their nests on rocky cliffs?

2. What would a sea bird use to build its nest on a rocky cliff?

3. How did Knocker know there was a dragon in the cave after reaching the second staircase?

4. Why could Jan understand Knocker and Megan sometimes, and not others?

5. What three things kept Megan from leaving the cave?

6. What three things happened to allow Megan to leave the cave?

7. Why did Megan return from Ituria's Island?

8. What types of predators (besides humans) would present a danger to sea birds and their chicks on the small rocky island cliffs? Are there different dangers to sea birds who live on sandy beach shores? Why?

9. Do you think some birds may have descended from dinosaurs?

10. How long is it from when a tern chick hatches until it can fly?

11. Something to think about: Because the Chinese Crested Tern was thought extinct for almost 100 years, there is truly little known about its habits. Scientists hope to put a tiny tracking device on an adult tern so they can track its activities and range during non-breeding season. Why is knowing where terns migrate to after breeding season and where they feed important to help save the species?

Discover more at
4HorsemenPublications.com

10% off using HORSEMEN10